This book is presented to:

Hannah Aicken

On the occasion of:

Christmas 2011

From:

Great Grandma Yon

The king is enthralled by your beauty;
honor him, for he is your lord.
Psalm 45:11

Princess with a Purpose™

By Kelly Chapman
Illustrated by Tammie Lyon

HARVEST HOUSE PUBLISHERS
EUGENE, OREGON

For my precious Kendall and all girls who want to know how to become a real princess.

Princess with a Purpose™

Text Copyright © 2010 by Kelly Chapman
Artwork Copyright © 2010 by Tammie Lyon

Published by Harvest House Publishers
Eugene, Oregon 97402
www.harvesthousepublishers.com

ISBN 978-0-7369-2435-1

Design and production by Mary pat Design, Westport, Connecticut

Printed in China

10 11 12 13 14 15 16 / LP / 10 9 8 7 6 5 4 3 2

What is Princess Prep School?
For more information, please visit
www.royalpurpose.com

Once upon a real time, there lived an eight-year-old girl
named Caroline who loved everything princess.
In her heart, she dreamed of one day becoming
a real princess, but in her mind, she knew
it was only make-believe.
Or was it?

"I can't wait to start the second-most-favorite day of my whole life, Nana!" Caroline said, bouncing out of bed to get ready for Princess Prep School. "I can't wait to be a real princess!"

"Then let's get ready," Nana told her granddaughter sweetly.

"Do you know what my first-most-favorite day is? It's the day that Jesus came to live in my heart."

"I remember," said Nana, "because it's my most-favorite day too."

"Hey! Don't leave without me," said Kendall, Caroline's four-year-old sister. Kendall loved everything that Caroline loved.

Caroline wished she and Kendall could arrive in a horse-drawn carriage. Instead, she and Kendall would get there in an ordinary car driven by Nana, whom they had lived with for as long as she could remember.

As Caroline and Kendall walked to their classroom, Caroline felt uneasy. Would she fit in? Could she ever be a real princess?

Caroline peeked inside and saw something that took her breath away. It was the most amazing trunk she had ever seen! Standing next to it was a lady who looked like an angel. Caroline watched as she opened the trunk and pulled out beautiful princess dresses. She even saw one that sparkled like a pink diamond.

Suddenly the classroom door flew open, and right in front of her stood . . .

"What are *you* doing here?" asked Prissy Crissy. "Don't you know that you need a king as your father and a queen as your mother to be a *real* princess?

"Hello, Caroline," said the pretty lady. "I'm Miss Lily, your Princess Prep School teacher. I'm glad you're here. Come and see the Trunk of Treasures. I think you'll find something special in it just for you!"

The girls gathered around Miss Lily. She taught them what it means to be a real princess. Everyone listened carefully except Caroline. She didn't feel very "princessy." All the other girls had a mommy and a daddy, but she and Kendall did not. This wasn't her second-most-favorite day after all.

That night Caroline prayed, "God, I love my Nana, but I need a mommy and daddy to be a real princess." Then Caroline cried until she fell fast asleep and started to dream.

In her dream, Caroline was dressed in her beautiful princess gown, she was at Princess Prep School, and her friends and Kendall were there.

Suddenly the King's helper entered the room. His name was Constant because he constantly forgot things and constantly spoke in rhyme.

"Oh, where did I put the royal invitation? Oh dear! Oh me! There will be no proclamation!" Constant mumbled.

11

"Are you looking for this?" asked Kendall, holding up a royal scroll.

"Yes, that's it! What a terrific find. Thank you, my dear. You are very kind," exclaimed Constant.

"Hear ye! Hear ye! Please come to a royal tea! We'd like you to meet a princess of Calvary. She will teach you how each one of you is blessed. We hope that you will join us and be our special guest."

A beautiful horse-drawn carriage came to take the girls to the castle. They couldn't believe it! They were going to a tea party to meet a real princess!

"Me first!" demanded Prissy Crissy, pushing her way to the front. "This is a surprise party my mommy and daddy planned for my birthday. I wanted a party with everything pretty, pink, and princess!"

Caroline was last in line. Her heart sank as she saw that there was no more room.

"Sorry, Caroline! I guess there's only room for real princesses," Prissy Crissy laughed.

"Oh skittle-dee-dee! Now let me see," said Constant, coming to her rescue. "I have a special place for you. Right up front, there's room for two!"

"Constant is my name, and serving is my aim," he continued with a bow. "I am the King's aide and His plans have all been made. Miss Caroline, please sit with me to see the Castle of Calvary."

"Yee-haw! What a great day for a tea party!" said a friendly country voice.

"Who said that?" asked Caroline.

"Miss Caroline, please meet the King's own royal horse. Keydon is his name. He will keep us all on course."

"A ta-ta-talking horse?" stuttered Caroline.

"Keydon is a horse who talks to us, of course. But he is wise and kind—a very friendly source," said Constant.

"Pleased to meet you, Caroline," said Keydon. "I'm glad you sat up front so I can tell you about the Prince of Calvary."

All the way to the castle, Caroline listened as Keydon told about the Prince's sacrifice for His royal subjects.

Trumpets blew as the huge castle doors opened. Miss Lily stepped forward. She was a Princess of Calvary!

"I've planned a wonderful day," Miss Lily said. "Let's hurry! I can't wait to show you the Castle of Calvary."

"That's easy-schmeasy!" cried Prissy Crissy. "A real princess belongs to a royal family. Her parents are the king and queen of the universe, and she has a gazillion maids who do whatever she wants." Prissy Crissy looked over her shoulder to see if Caroline was listening.

"That's not quite correct," Princess Lily said sweetly.

"A real princess," interrupted Prissy Crissy, "wears a pretty crown and lovely dresses. And she is beautiful—just like me!"

"You are beautiful," Princess Lily replied, "but the way you look and the dresses you wear don't make you a real princess. Look at the pretty pink flowers on the table. In a few days, they won't be beautiful anymore. Outside beauty fades away, but real beauty comes from inside your heart."

"A real princess has a heart full of love for her King and others. That's what makes her truly beautiful."

"I don't believe it!" shouted Prissy Crissy. "Loving others can't be more important than the pretty dresses I wear!"

"It's true," said Princess Lily. "A real princess has a heart filled with love."

"Doesn't a real princess have to be a king's daughter?" asked Caroline, hoping she was wrong.

"Yes," cried Princess Lily, "but not just a king. He has to be the King of kings!"

"Prissy Crissy was right!" cried Caroline. "I don't have a father, so I can't ever become a real princess."

"Caroline! Is that why you've been sad?" Princess Lily asked. "You've been thinking about your earthly father instead of your heavenly Father."

"My heavenly Father?" Caroline asked.

"Remember when you first believed that Jesus died on the cross for all the bad things you've done?"

Caroline nodded.

25

"You became a real princess the moment you believed Jesus died on the cross for your sins and was raised to life again. And since He is the King of kings and you are His daughter, that makes you His . . ."

"Princess? I'm a *real* princess?" Caroline cried. She'd been a real princess all along. With Jesus in her heart, she was a daughter of the King of kings!

"I don't know how to be a real princess," Caroline said. "I want to know everything about who I am to Jesus and be the princess He wants me to be!"

"Sweet Caroline, this is cause for a Royal Celebration!" Trumpets blared as Constant appeared, carrying a sparkling crown.

"Daughter of the King, because you understand the truth, I present you with a Truth Tiara," said Princess Lily, proudly placing the crown on Caroline's head.

"It's more beautiful than I ever dreamed!" exclaimed Caroline.

27

The girls were excited about Caroline's new crown—all except Prissy Crissy. She was upset because she didn't have one. But before she could complain, it was time to go home.

Constant announced the carriage had arrived. Princess Lily and the girls hugged and said good-bye.

"Princess Lily, may I keep my Truth Tiara?" Caroline asked.

"Absolutely!" she replied. "May it remind you that you are a real princess of the King of kings."

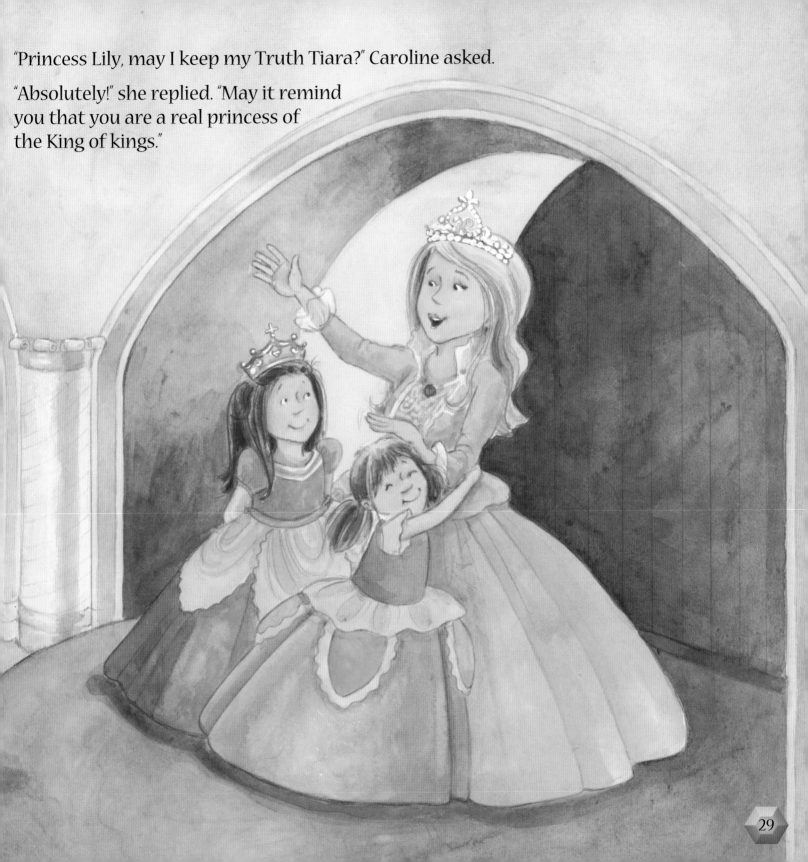

"Wake up my sleepy head! It's time for my princess to get out of bed," Caroline's grandmother sang.

Caroline sat up straight and joyfully shouted, "I really am a princess!"

How do I become a daughter of the King?

It's easy to say and do things to make the people you love happy. Becoming a daughter of the King is much more than that! You must truly love Jesus with all of your heart and, because of that love, you must really want to connect with Him in a genuine relationship that happens because of how much you love Him. That's when God becomes your Father in heaven and you know that you are a daughter of the King!

You must believe that Jesus died on the cross for your sins and that He was raised again three days later. Sins are the bad things we do. They are things like disobeying and being selfish.

> *For God so loved the world that he gave his one and only Son, that whoever believes in him shall not perish but have eternal life.—John 3:16*

Then you pray and ask Jesus into your heart, not just so you can be a real princess, but because you love Him and believe He died for you.

> *If you confess with your mouth, "Jesus is Lord," and believe in your heart that God raised him from the dead, you will be saved.—Romans 10:9*

The moment you pray and ask Jesus into your heart as Lord and Savior, you become a real princess!

> *"I will be a Father to you, and you will be my sons and daughters," says the Lord Almighty.—2 Corinthians 6:18*

You will also live happily-ever-after in eternity with Jesus one day.

> *For the wages of sin is death, but the gift of God is eternal life in Christ Jesus our Lord.—Romans 6:23*

A Princess Prayer

Dear Jesus,
I know that I have sin in my life because I have chosen to do some wrong things. I know I can't make up for this just by doing good things. I know that I need You to take my sin away. I believe You died on the cross for me, that You rose again, and now I am forgiven. I want You to be Lord of my life. Thank You, Jesus, for coming to live in my heart. I am now a daughter of the King of kings!

Hear ye! Hear ye!

Let it be known throughout the land,

Princess_____

is now part of God's royal plan!

For she believed and now Jesus lives in her heart,

where He will live forever and never depart.

She also believes He died on the cross for her sins

and then three days later, He rose again.

The date she believed, _____,

whereupon the angels did sing, was the day

they celebrated her becoming a daughter of the King!